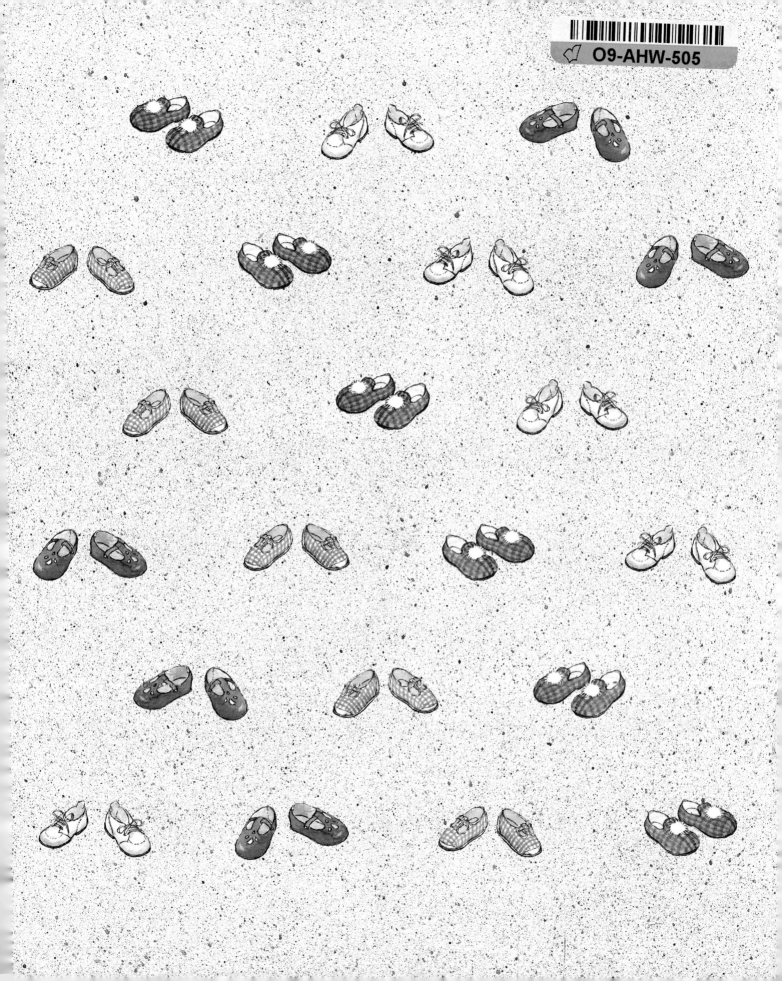

For Mara and Marissa
M.W.

For Sarah, Rowan, Rachel,
Helen, Sarah W., and Charlie . . .
giants to be.
P.D.

Text copyright © 1989 by Martin Waddell
Illustrations copyright © 1989 by Penny Dale

Second U.S. edition 1995

Library of Congress Cataloging-in-Publication Data

Waddell, Martin.
Once there were giants / Martin Waddell ;
illustrated by Penny Dale.—2nd U.S. ed.
Summary: As a baby girl grows up and becomes an adult,
the "giants" in her family seem to grow smaller.
ISBN 1-56402-612-4
[1. Growth—Fiction.   2. Family life—Fiction.]
I. Dale, Penny, ill. II. Title.
PZ7.W1137On   1995
[E]—dc20   94-40021

2 4 6 8 10 9 7 5 3 1

Printed in Hong Kong

The pictures in this book were done in watercolor and pencil crayon.

Candlewick Press
2067 Massachusetts Avenue
Cambridge, Massachusetts 02140

Once There Were
GIANTS

Martin Waddell

illustrated by Penny Dale

CANDLEWICK PRESS
CAMBRIDGE, MASSACHUSETTS

Once there were giants in our house.
There were Mom and Dad and
Jill and John and Uncle Tom.

The small one on the rug is me.

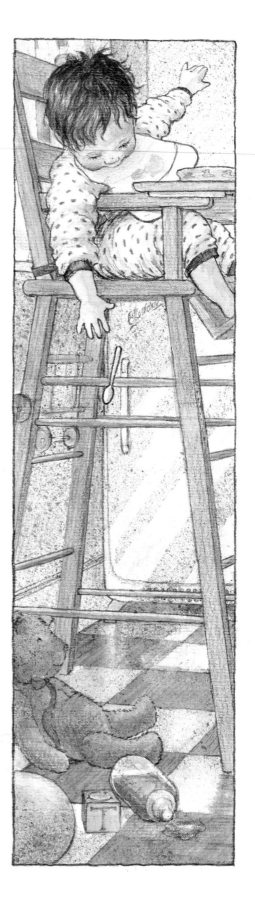

When I could sit up

Mom bought me a high chair.

I sat at the table

way up in the sky

with Mom and Dad and

Jill and John and Uncle Tom.

The one throwing oatmeal is me.

When I could crawl

I crawled around on the floor.

Dad was a dragon and

he gave a roar that scared

Jill and John and Uncle Tom.

The one who is crying is me.

When I could walk

I walked to the park with

Jill and John and Uncle Tom.

We fed the ducks and

Jill stood on her head.

The one in the duck pond is me.

When I could talk
I talked and talked!
I annoyed Uncle Tom and
was sat on by Jill and by John.
That's John on my head
and Jill on my knee.

The one on my bottom is me!

When I could run
I ran and ran,
chased by Mom and Dad
and Uncle Tom and
Jill on her bike and
my brother John.

The one out of breath is me.

When I went to play group
I wouldn't play games and
I called people names and
spilled the water on Millie Magee.
She's the one with the towel.

The one being lectured is me!

When I went to school
I'd gotten bigger by then.
Mom had to leave at
a quarter to ten and
she didn't come back
for a long, long time.
I didn't shout and
I didn't scream.
She came for me at
a quarter to three.

The one on Mom's knee is me.

When I went to grade school

I had lots of fun.

I got big and strong

and punched my brother John.

He's the one with the sore nose.

The one with the black eye is me.

When I went to high school
I was taller than Mom,
and almost as tall as my uncle Tom.
But I never caught up
with my brother John.
I ran and I jumped
and they all came to see.
There they are cheering.

The one who's just winning is me.

When I went to work
I lived all by myself.
Then I met Don and we got married.
There's Jill and John
and Uncle Tom
and Mom's the one crying,
and Dad is the one
with the beer on his head.

The bride looking happy is me!

Then we had a baby girl
and things changed.
There are giants in our house again!
There is my husband, Don,
and Jill and John,
my mom and my dad
and Uncle Tom
and one of the giants is . . .

ME!

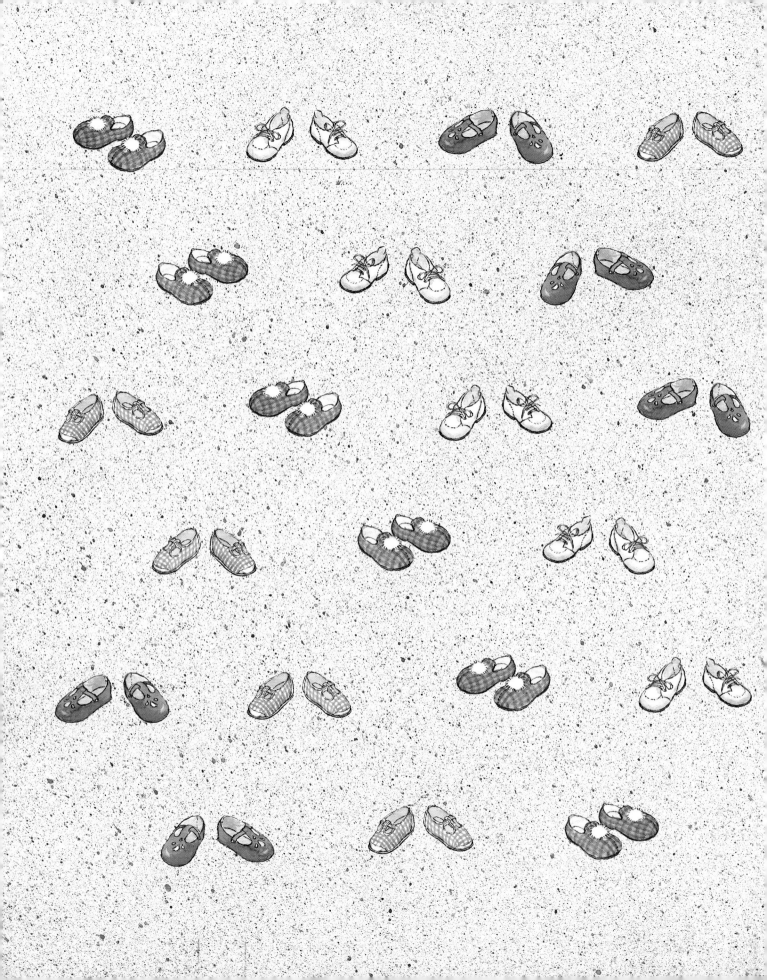